Dear Parent:
Your child's love of reading starts here!

Every child learns to read in a different way and at his or her own speed. Some go back and forth between reading levels and read favorite books again and again. Others read through each level in order. You can help your young reader improve and become more confident by encouraging his or her own interests and abilities. From books your child reads with you to the first books he or she reads alone, there are I Can Read Books for every stage of reading:

SHARED READING
Basic language, word repetition, and whimsical illustrations, ideal for sharing with your emergent reader

BEGINNING READING
Short sentences, familiar words, and simple concepts for children eager to read on their own

READING WITH HELP
Engaging stories, longer sentences, and language play for developing readers

READING ALONE
Complex plots, challenging vocabulary, and high-interest topics for the independent reader

ADVANCED READING
Short paragraphs, chapters, and exciting themes for the perfect bridge to chapter books

I Can Read Books have introduced children to the joy of reading since 1957. Featuring award-winning authors and illustrators and a fabulous cast of beloved characters, I Can Read Books set the standard for beginning readers.

A lifetime of discovery begins with the magical words **"I Can Read!"**

Visit www.icanread.com for information
on enriching your child's reading experience.

For Collin
—L.M.S.

For Alex
—S.K.H.

Happy Halloween, Mittens Text copyright © 2010 by Lola M. Schaefer Illustrations copyright © 2010 by Susan Kathleen Hartung All rights reserved. Manufactured in China. No part of this book may be used or reproduced in any manner whatsoever without written permission except in the case of brief quotations embodied in critical articles and reviews. For information address HarperCollins Children's Books, a division of HarperCollins Publishers, 10 East 53rd Street, New York, NY 10022. www.icanread.com

Library of Congress Cataloging-in-Publication Data
Schaefer, Lola M., date
  Happy Halloween, Mittens / story by Lola M. Schaefer ; pictures by Susan Kathleen Hartung. — 1st ed.
    p. cm. — (My first I can read)
  Summary: While Nick prepares for Halloween, Mittens the kitten tries his best to help out.
  ISBN 978-0-06-170222-8 (trade bdg.) — ISBN 978-0-06-170221-1 (pbk.)
  [1. Cats—Fiction. 2. Animals—Infancy—Fiction. 3. Halloween—Fiction.] I. Hartung, Susan Kathleen, ill. II. Title.
PZ7.S33233Hap 2010   2008045065
[E]—dc22   CIP
                                                                                           AC

10 11 12 13 14 SCP 10 9 8 7 6 5 4 3 2 1   ❖   First Edition

I Can Read!™

SHARED My First READING

Happy Halloween, Mittens

story by **Lola M. Schaefer**

pictures by **Susan Kathleen Hartung**

HARPER
An Imprint of HarperCollinsPublishers

Nick is getting ready
for Halloween.
Mittens wants to help.

Nick paints spooky faces.

Mittens paints faces, too.

"Oh, Mittens," says Nick.
"You are not helping!"

Nick puts up
a spooky cobweb.

Mittens puts up a cobweb,
too.

Oops!

The cobweb falls down
on Mittens.

"Oh, Mittens," says Nick.
"You are not helping!"

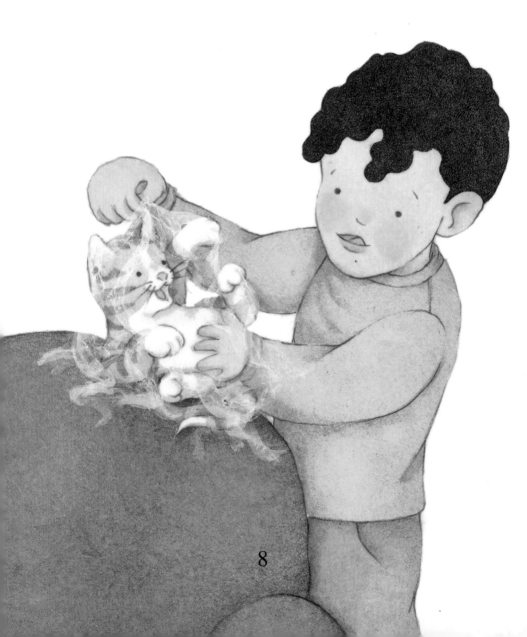

Nick makes spooky cookies.

Mittens makes cookies, too.

"Oh, Mittens," says Nick.

"You are not helping at all!"

Mittens runs away.

Mittens licks

and licks

and licks.

Soon, he is clean and fluffy.

Mittens still wants to help.

Mittens finds Nick
on the porch.

Nick hangs a ghost.

The ghost blows in the wind.

"This ghost is not spooky,"
says Nick.
"I don't know what to do!"

Nick watches the ghost.

Mittens watches the ghost, too.

He jumps up.

The ghost blows past Mittens.

Mittens bats the ghost.

Scratch!

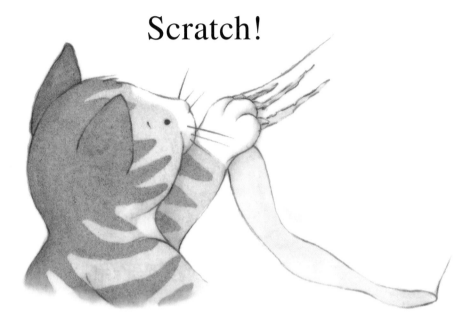

Mittens bats the ghost again.

Scratch!

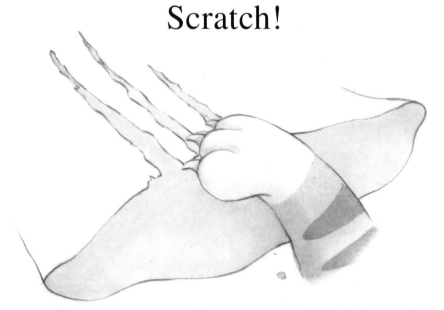

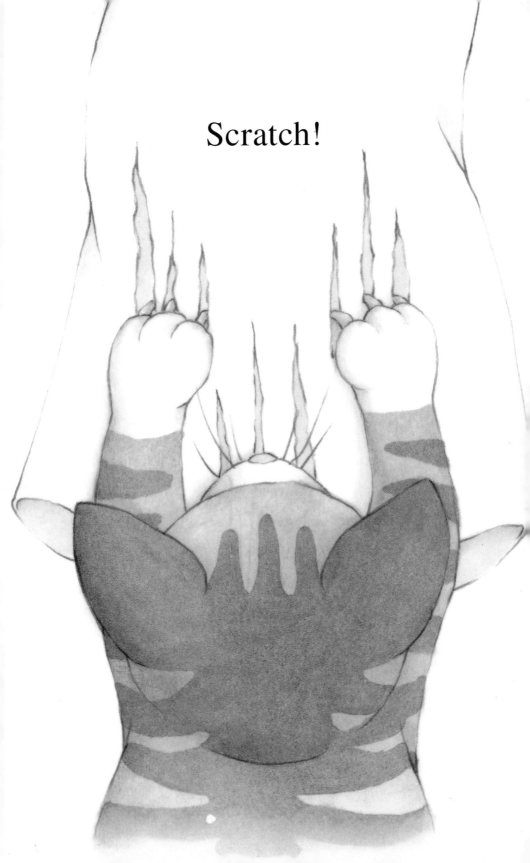

Mittens moves away.
A spooky ghost blows
in the wind.

"Thank you for helping,
Mittens," says Nick.
"Now we are ready
for Halloween!"

23

Boo!

Meow!